Bode gets a Job

Dr. Bobby Moore

Book Design & Production: Columbus Publishing Lab • www.ColumbusPublishingLab.com

Paperback ISBN: 978-1-63337-256-6
Hardback ISBN: 978-1-63337-257-3
E-book ISBN: 978-1-63337-258-0

Printed in the United States of America 1 3 5 7 9 10 8 6 4 2

Dedicated to all the children who love to read and who love animals. A special dedication goes to my wife, as well as Bode and all my friends and colleagues who helped me during my diagnosis with multiple myeloma.

Once you have a wonderful dog,
a life without one is a life diminished.

—Author unknown

Airport Security Dog

Bode, Bode,
Smells passengers' luggage as they go by,
Ensuring everyone is safe
When they get on the plane to fly.

Airport security dogs have become a common sight at airports. The canine teams (dog + handler) are usually near the security lines checking passengers' luggage. The dogs can be trained to smell and detect a variety of objects. Some are trained to sniff for explosives or bombs. Some are trained to sniff and detect drugs. Some dogs are trained to sniff for fruit that travelers may have with them as they are coming into the country, or leaving the country to go to another country. Some dogs are even trained to smell money to keep people from bringing fake currency into the country.

When you see an airport security dog, it is very important not to approach the dog or try to pet him. These dogs are specifically trained for their work, and are not used to people approaching or petting them. Many airport security dogs wear vests that read "do not pet." We should be very appreciative of the hard-working dogs at the airport, as they help ensure that passengers are safe and can fly in friendly skies.

Service Dog

Bode, Bode,
Has really strong paws,
To assist those in need
Is his valiant cause.

A service dog is trained to assist individuals with disabilities. Service dogs can bring a sense of joy and freedom to their owners. A person partnered with a service dog has full public access rights as granted by federal law (the Americans with Disabilities Act), which allows them to take their dogs into all public facilities. As a result, service dogs are never separated from their human partners!

Police Dog

Bode, Bode,
So brave and strong.
He helps keep you safe
From those who do wrong.

Dogs have been used to help sniff out criminals for more than 200 years. Dogs were also used in World War I and World War II, and you often see them in movies and shows about the police or military.

A police dog's nose is about fifty times more sensitive than a human's nose. Police dogs can sniff out drugs, bombs, and weapons that humans cannot find. Not every dog can be a police dog. Most police dogs are male German Shepherds, but any large dog that is smart, aggressive, and strong like Bode could be a good candidate.

Guard Dog

Bode, Bode,
Always on alert.
If you try anything "funny"
He might grab your shirt.

A guard dog or watch dog is used to help protect people, places, and things. When a guard dog sees or smells something peculiar, the dog may bark loudly to alert its owners, trainers, or handlers. Many times the guard dog's bark may scare the intruder away. Sometimes the guard dog may corner or capture an intruder.

Guard dogs come in a variety of shapes and sizes. As long as a dog is well trained to alert its owner when there is danger, a good guard dog may be a variety of breeds. Bode would make a great guard dog.

Hunting Dog

Bode, Bode,
Loves to retrieve.
He will bring you the "game"
You expect to receive.

Bode is a Vizsla, which is a breed of dog that is sometimes known as the Hungarian Pointer. These dogs were originally used to hunt, point, and retrieve. They were first bred in Hungary.

Vizsla are referred to as "velcro dogs." They love to be close to their owners and lay on their laps. This is a trait that was bred years ago when hunters wanted their dogs to be close to them and not roam too far away. Bode loves to retrieve things and he loves to lie on your lap.

Water Rescue Dog

Bode, Bode,
Jumps right in.
He'll come to save you
If you can't swim.

Rescue dogs are real heroes. They save many lives every year and work with the police, military, and coast guard. There are dogs that are helicopter trained and will even parachute out of planes with their handlers. Water rescue dogs go through a lot of training to be comfortable in and out of the water.

Show Dog

Bode, Bode,
He's the best.
In shows like this
He puffs out his chest.

Many people raise dogs just to enter them into dog shows and contests. Showing dogs is a great sport where the thrill of competition is combined with the joy of seeing beautiful dogs. Some of these competitions will draw millions of viewers on TV. When dogs compete in these shows, there are awards for all types of breeds. Show dogs are beautiful animals and are always well kept, groomed, and trained. Although Bode is not a show dog, he is beautiful.

Avalanche Dog

Bode, Bode,
Will do whatever you want him to do.
Bode would be a great choice
To be a dog for Search and Rescue.

Avalanche Dogs (Search and Rescue/SAR) are trained to smell the human scent. These dogs can be used in a variety of disasters where humans may be in grave danger. SAR dogs are typically trained to find humans in the wilderness, building collapses, earthquakes, landslides, and avalanches. The training to become an SAR dog is very rigorous. The training starts when a puppy is eight to ten weeks old. The dogs go through obedience training, agility training, and scent training several hours each week. Bode loves the snow just like his human.

Sled Dog

Bode, Bode,
Sits home and dreams,
That if he lived in Alaska
He could be part of a dog sled team.

While sled dogs are now mostly used for recreation and racing, there was a time when they were very important for exploration. During exploration of the North and South Poles, sled dog teams carried supplies, equipment, and medicine. Most sled dogs are Huskies, as they are strong and have thick fur that keeps them warm. Sled dogs are still used in many areas of Alaska and Canada. One of the most famous dog sled races is the Iditarod Trail Sled Dog Race in Alaska, which covers the distance from Anchorage to Nome. The race takes more than eight days and is very challenging for the dog sled teams.

Herd Dog

Bode, Bode,
Loves his sheep.
He keeps them safe
Without a peep.

Herding other animals is a trait many dogs are born with, but it can also be developed through training. Some dogs are "headers" and stay in the front of the pack, while other dogs are "heelers" and will stay near the back of the herd. Dogs will herd either by barking, biting at the heel of another animal, or by using their own bodies to nudge the herd in the desired direction.

Owners can measure the herding instincts of their dogs when they are around livestock or other animals. Just like there are contests for show dogs and sled dogs, there are also contests for herding dogs.

Movie Star Dog

Bode, Bode,
He's a star.
On cue he can jump
From a burning car!

Nearly everyone has seen a movie or TV show with a dog. There used to be a very famous TV show called *Lassie,* in which a dog and her owner, Timmy, would have adventures every week in front of one million viewers. All dogs used in movies are well trained. Sometimes in a movie they will use several different dogs to play just one part. Movie crews do this because each dog may be trained for specific skills. Some dogs may be better jumpers, better swimmers, or perform better on command. Movie dogs seldom get hurt while filming, and are kept safe and healthy by their owners and handlers.

Bode, Bode,
You are a special breed.
The best job for you
Is teaching children to read!

While there may be lots of exciting jobs for Bode, there is one that he loves the most. His favorite job is visiting schools and helping students get excited about reading. When students are strong readers, they can become anything in the world. Learning to read is a pathway to an exciting life.

DR. BOBBY MOORE is known for high energy, engaging, and thought-provoking keynote addresses, presentations, and workshops. Moore has presented all over the country and internationally. As the former principal of a nationally recognized middle school and the author of two AMLE books 1) Culture Starts with You and 2) Inspire, Motivate, Collaborate, he is recognized across the country as a thought leader in education. While serving as middle school principal, his school received visitors from all over the state to learn how one of the lowest funded districts in Ohio was also one of the highest performing, despite poverty and limited resources. During his time as a superintendent Bobby led his district to the highest rating of Excellent with Distinction, the very first time for the district, and to a ranking among the top districts in the state for student growth.

For the last several years, Bobby led one of the largest school improvement collaboratives in the United States for the not-for-profit Battelle for Kids and has done extensive consulting with state departments of education and large urban districts. Bobby is currently president and CEO of the EPIC Impact Education Group and is the strategic partnerships and professional learning manager for AMLE. His areas of interest and expertise include leadership; emotional intelligence; high performing middle schools; positive school culture; motivating and engaging staff; leveraging time, talent, and resources (school scheduling); literacy; and character education. When he is not traveling the world speaking or presenting, he is spending time with his faithful and loving companion Bode.

Follow Bobby Moore on Twitter: @DrBobbyMoore

www.EPICImpactedgroup.com